OCT 1994

Jₚ

Newman, Al.

Grub E. Dog /

Grub E. Dog

By Al Newman

Illustrated by Jim Doody

Publisher's Cataloging in Publication
(Prepared by Quality Books Inc.)

Newman, Alfred T.
 Grub E. Dog / by Al Newman; illustrated by Jim Doody.
  p. cm.
  Audience: Ages 3 through 9
  SUMMARY: Grub E. Dog is a big messy dog who can't keep either
himself or his room clean. Readers can help him learn to be neat
and orderly.
  Preassigned LCCN: 93-77686.
  ISBN 0-89334-214-9 (hard.)
  ISBN 0-89334-218-1 (pbk.)

 1. Dogs—Juvenile fiction. 2. Hygiene—Juvenile fiction. 3. Dogs—Fiction. 4.
Cleanliness—Fiction. I. Doody, James J., ill. II. Title.

PZ7 .N4953G78 1993   [E]
                                                   QBI93-547

Humanics Children's House
P.O. Box 7400
Atlanta, GA 30357
Humanics Children's House is an imprint of Humanics Limited.

Grub E. Dog is
a hopeless case.

He never cleans up.

Just look at this place!

He won't brush his teeth.

He won't wash his ears.

His friends hold their
noses whenever he's near.

His bed is never made.

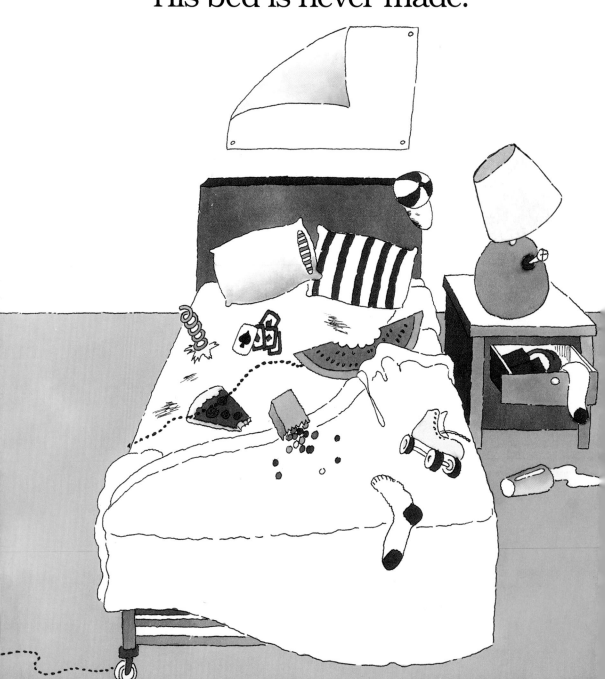

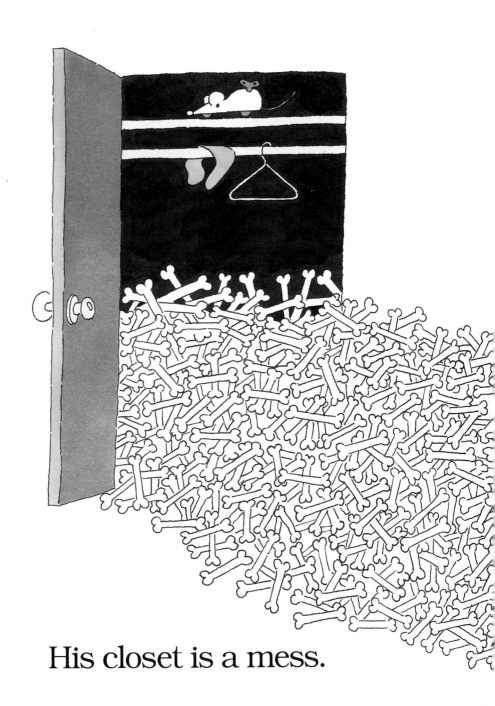

His closet is a mess.

He leaves his clothes
on the floor,

and he couldn't care less.

This dog needs your help!

You can show him
what to do.

Then he'll always
be your friend.

And you'll be
his friend too.

Show him how
to comb his hair
and wash his face.

Teach him to hang
all his clothes
in their proper place.

and make his bed
every day.

Remind him
to put all
his toys away.

Teach Grub E. Dog
to stay neat and clean . . .

wear a big smile,

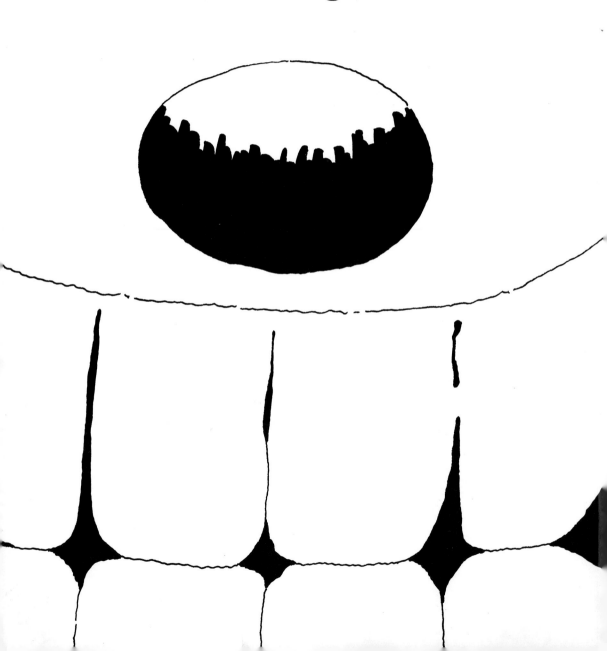

and never be mean.

Then he'll have
lots of friends

and plenty of fun.

Give Grub E. a bone for a job well done!